For Frank and Amanda
~ *C.L.*

For Mum and Dad
~ *J.M.*

First published in 1997 by Magi Publications
22 Manchester Street, London W1M 5PG

This edition published 1997

Text © 1997 Christine Leeson
Illustrations © 1997 Joanne Moss

Christine Leeson and Joanne Moss have asserted their rights
to be identified as the author and illustrator of this work under
the Copyright, Designs and Patents Act, 1988.

Printed and bound in Belgium by Proost NV, Turnhout

ISBN 1 85430 423 2

Crafty
Little Freddie

by Christine Leeson

illustrated by Joanne Moss

One crisp, star-frosted night Mrs Fox gathered her three cubs together outside the den.

"I think it's time you all learned to hunt," she told them. "Tonight you can try to catch your own suppers."

Frannie and Rennie were very excited. They frisked and jumped and tore off into the woods to stalk mice. But they were clumsy and noisy and they didn't catch a single one. Rennie even got bitten on the nose!

"*I'm* not catching any silly mice," said Freddie. "I'm much too clever to bother with all that chasing. I'll let my supper come to me."

Freddie trotted briskly through the woods until he reached the road. His mother had often told him to stay away, but Freddie knew there were sometimes tasty treats by the side of it. A car sped past. Something pale and fluttering flew out of its window and landed at Freddie's feet.

Was it alive?

It didn't move but it smelt delicious. It even *tasted* delicious.

"There, what did I say!" cried Freddie. "A lovely supper and no work. What a crafty little fox I am!" And feeling very pleased with himself, he trotted home.

"Well, how did you get on?" asked Mrs Fox, when the cubs returned to the den.
Freddie stepped proudly forward with his catch.
"That's *human's* food!" cried Mrs Fox. She glared at Freddie but she couldn't be cross for long.
There wasn't much meat on the worm and the beetle that Frannie and Rennie had caught. It was very clever of Freddie to find the tastiest supper of all.

The next morning, Mrs Fox sent
her cubs off again. This time Frannie
and Rennie hunted pigeons but the big
birds easily flapped out of their way
and perched in the trees. Frannie tried
to climb after them.

Freddie laughed like anything when
Frannie got stuck and Rennie tried to
help her down again.
"What idiots!" he said. "All that hard
work for nothing. As for me, I'll find
myself another easy meal."

Freddie wandered on down to the river bank.
A fisherman sat there, with a tempting picnic basket
by his side.
"Delicious!" thought the young fox, licking his lips.
He waited until the fisherman had dozed off and then
he craftily crept up to the basket and grabbed the food.
Just in time!
As Freddie sneaked away, the fisherman yawned and
opened his eyes.

"You tried your best," Mrs Fox told Frannie and Rennie when the cubs returned to the den. They had brought her a snail and a tail feather.

"Look what I've got!" said Freddie.

"That isn't *prey*!" cried Mrs Fox. "You didn't hunt it."

"I sneaked up on it ever so quietly," said Freddie. "It nearly got away."

"You're too crafty for your own good," said Mrs Fox. "You'll be in big trouble one day, you mark my words!"

The next evening Mrs Fox sent the cubs out to catch rabbits. Off went Frannie and Rennie into the fields, where the rabbits' white bobtails shone like stars in the dusk.

Frannie followed one of them down a rabbit hole and got stuck. Rennie had to pull her out by the tail.

"Stupid things!" thought Freddie. "I'm not going to waste my time catching rabbits. *I* know where there's even juicier food."

Off Freddie trotted towards the farmyard.
He peered through the fence and could see a nice,
plump gosling, sitting in a pool of bright moonlight.
"Yummy!" said Freddie. "Just waiting for me."
Very quietly, he crawled towards the gosling . . .

one step . . .

two steps . . .

three steps . . .

At that moment, everything happened at once.
The gosling squealed. The farmyard dog barked,
and all the other geese came running towards him,
hissing and honking and snapping.
Freddie looked for a way of escape. He saw a gap
and ran out through the gate, as fast as his four paws
could carry him.

Freddie ran and ran until he reached the woods.
The geese and the dog were close behind him
and Freddie thought his last moment had come.
But then something happened.

A streak of red fur
launched itself on
the pursuing animals,
barking and snarling.
There was a flurry
of fur and feathers
and before Freddie
knew what was happening,
Mrs Fox ran out from the fighting mass.
"Run, you silly little fox, run!" she cried.
Freddie and his mother both ran and ran until the
noise of the geese and the dog was
far behind them.

A little later, Freddie and his mother arrived back at the den.

"What have you caught?" asked Frannie.

"Freddie nearly got caught himself," said Mrs Fox, as she told them what had happened.

"Stupid Freddie!" laughed Rennie and Frannie. "Serves you right for being too clever."

"You're not as crafty as you think you are," scolded Mrs Fox. "Off you go to bed now, before you get into any more trouble!"

Freddie crept quietly into the corner of the den to sleep and was soon hunting again –
but only in his dreams.